For Helen with love
S.H.

For Christle, Mimi, Ruth and Didi
H.C.

Fun-to-Read Picture Books have been
grouped into three approximate readability
levels by Bernice Moon, teacher-in-charge,
Ellington Language and Literacy Centre,
Maidenhead, Berkshire. Yellow books
are suitable for beginners; red books
for readers acquiring first fluency; blue
books for more advanced readers.

This book has been assessed as Stage 7
according to *Individualised Reading*, by
Cliff Moon and Norman Ruel, published by
the Reading and Language Information Centre,
University of Reading.

First published 1988 by
Walker Books Ltd
87 Vauxhall Walk
London SE11 5HJ

Text © 1988 Sarah Hayes
Illustrations © 1988 Helen Craig

First printed 1988
Printed and bound in Italy by L.E.G.O., Vicenza

British Library Cataloguing in Publication Data
Hayes, Sarah
This is the bear and the picnic lunch. — (Fun-to-read picture books)
I. Title   II. Craig, Helen   III. Series
823'.914[J]   PZ7

ISBN 0-7445-0555-0

THIS IS THE
BEAR
AND THE
PICNIC LUNCH

WRITTEN BY

Sarah Hayes

ILLUSTRATED BY

Helen Craig

WALKER BOOKS
LONDON

This is the boy
who packed a lunch

of sandwiches, crisps and
an apple to crunch.

This is the bear
who guarded the box

while the boy went to find

his shoes and socks.

This is the dog
who sneaked past the chair

towards the lunch and
the brave guard bear.

This is the bear
with his eyes half closed
who did not notice
the dog's black nose.

This is the bear
who was sound asleep

when the dog performed
a tremendous leap…

on to the table...

down to the floor...

and off to hide

behind the door...

and all that he left
of the picnic lunch
was an empty box and
the apple to crunch.

This is the boy
who looked everywhere

for his lunch and his dog
and his brave guard bear.

This is the boy
who heard the munch

of a dog and a bear
eating picnic lunch.

This is the boy
who tried to be angry

but found he was
suddenly terribly hungry.

This is the boy
who packed a new lunch
of sandwiches, crisps and
the apple to crunch.
And this is the bear who said,
"Haven't you guessed?
Indoor picnics are the best!"